Me the Tree

Rich Mullaney

Illustrator: Amanda Pfeiffer

Balboa Press books may be ordered through booksellers or by contacting:

Balboa Press
A Division of Hay House
1663 Liberty Drive
Bloomington, IN 47403
www.balboapress.com
1 (877) 407-4847

Because of the dynamic nature of the Internet, any web addresses or links contained in this book may have changed since publication and may no longer be valid. The views expressed in this work are solely those of the author and do not necessarily reflect the views of the publisher, and the publisher hereby disclaims any responsibility for them.

Any people depicted in stock imagery provided by Getty Images are models, and such images are being used for illustrative purposes only.
Certain stock imagery © Getty Images.

Illustrator: Amanda Pfeiffer
Photographer: Daisha Riofrio

ISBN: 978-1-9822-4092-9 (sc)
ISBN: 978-1-9822-4093-6 (e)

Library of Congress Control Number: 2020900425

Print information available on the last page.

Balboa Press rev. date: 01/08/2020

Me the Tree

M Y FIRST MEMORY WAS CLINGING to my mother, a grand cottonwood tree. I was high in the air. It was a warm spring morning. A light breeze came by and carried me high in the sky and I enjoyed a morning ride tumbling on the breeze.

EVENTUALLY MY COTTONY SIDES GOT caught on a piece of grass. This is where I hung for several days until a big rainstorm washed me down into the soil.

I STAYED THERE FOR A VERY long time.

THE SOIL SURROUNDING ME STARTED warming and I had an urge to stretch and noticed that I was breaking through the hard shell that surrounded and protected me. I felt branches growing from me

and pushing upwards to the sky and roots working their way down. As my branches broke through the soil surface, I felt the sunshine. The sunshine was giving me energy and strength. I felt buds growing and forming large leaves. I was struggling, pushing and shoving other plants around me. It seems like we were all wanting the same thing, sun on our leaves and strong long roots to reach for water and food in the soil.

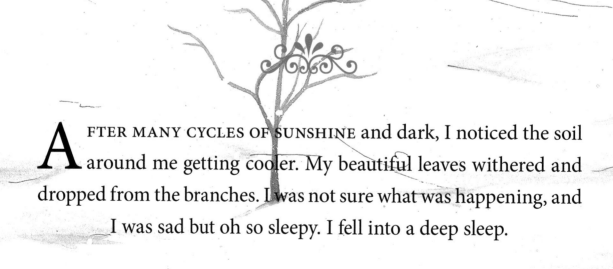

A FTER MANY CYCLES OF SUNSHINE and dark, I noticed the soil around me getting cooler. My beautiful leaves withered and dropped from the branches. I was not sure what was happening, and I was sad but oh so sleepy. I fell into a deep sleep.

A s the soil started warming, I slowly awoke. I felt buds forming on my branches. The buds burst into leaves and reached for the sun. As my beautiful leaves capture the sunshine, I felt energy move through me.

I WAS TALLER THAN MOST OF the plants around now and did not need to fight as hard for the sunshine. Each day I was growing taller and stronger. All too soon I felt the soil getting colder and I was getting oh-so sleepy. Again, I fell into a deep sleep.

DURING MY THIRD CYCLE, AS the soil started getting warmer, I woke from my slumber and again started reaching for the sun and my roots started growing deeper.

D URING THIS YEAR I WAS tall enough to see my surroundings. I started noticing animals wandering by me. Squirrels were busy chasing each other and chattering.

INSECTS WERE BUSY FLYING HERE and there. Birds were singing and gathering small stems and branches for their nests. I continued to gather sunshine and grew even taller. I realized that growing when the soil was warm and sleeping when the soil was cold was the cycle of growing.

BY MY TENTH CYCLE, A couple of robins built a nest in my branches. I was so proud to finally earn the trust of holding a bird family for the year. I became more and more observant of the abundance of life all around me.

I SHIVERED IN SHOCK LATER IN my tenth cycle as I encountered whispers dancing on my leaves. The robins told me, "Those are lyrics of Angels. If you relax and concentrate you will hear their true songs". I did as the robins suggested. After several days the whispers turned into very beautiful voices. The Angels sang "Oh wonderful Cottonwood we are Angels created to provide guidance. We ask that we may live with you, so we are available to all who travel past and request our assistance." The prayer was filled with love and I openly accepted. Immediately I felt the essence of their love as they spread their wings throughout my leaves.

Several cycles later as my buds were starting to emerge, I felt a wonderful tickle on my branches. It was a joyful feeling filled with laughter. As I did with the Angels, I relaxed and concentrated. Slowly, I became aware of jubilant little beings wandering throughout my branches. These little beings were so excited as I woke to their vibrations. As the leader came forward, he buzzed, "Oh majestic Cottonwood, we are Tree Fairies. We live within trees. Last winter our companion tree was blown over in a storm and is slowing cycling its life nutrients back into the earth. We have come to request your permission to live with you. We build beautiful houses and in return spread the fun and joy for many miles." These words were filled with much joy and laughter and it created a strong desire to have these Fairies in my life.

Sharing my universe with Angels and Tree Fairies created a wonderful life. They openly shared their gifts with any who asked.

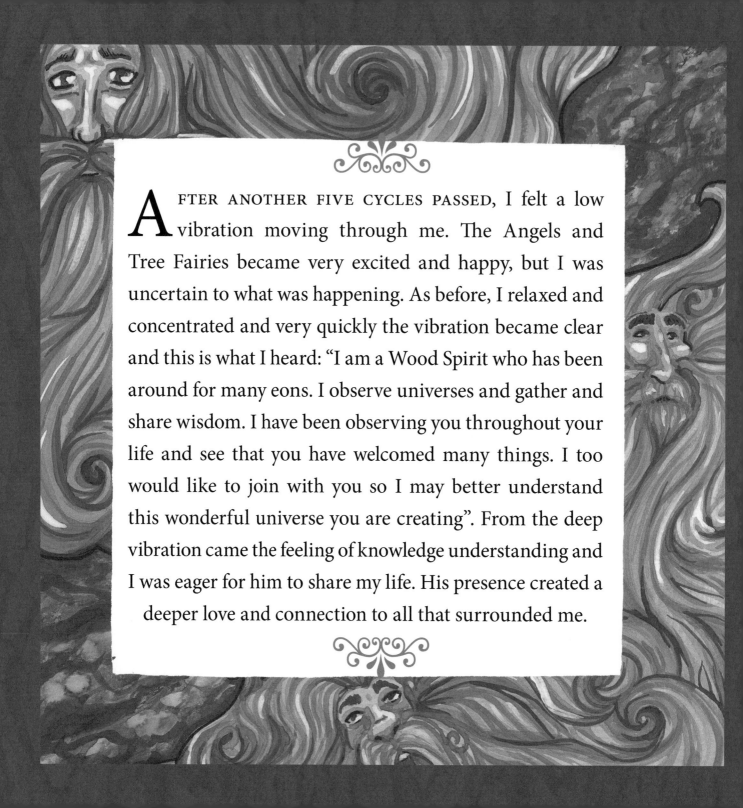

After another five cycles passed, I felt a low vibration moving through me. The Angels and Tree Fairies became very excited and happy, but I was uncertain to what was happening. As before, I relaxed and concentrated and very quickly the vibration became clear and this is what I heard: "I am a Wood Spirit who has been around for many eons. I observe universes and gather and share wisdom. I have been observing you throughout your life and see that you have welcomed many things. I too would like to join with you so I may better understand this wonderful universe you are creating". From the deep vibration came the feeling of knowledge understanding and I was eager for him to share my life. His presence created a deeper love and connection to all that surrounded me.

OVERTIME, I KNEW I WAS not just a tree. I was one with Angels, Tree Fairies, Wood Spirits, and the surrounding plants and animals. I was one with the Universe that was connected to all the surroundings.

Oh!! How beautiful and loving this universe is.

I knew someday that as a tree I would no longer exist in the physical world, but this Universe would continue to expand. However, the core part of the Wood Spirits, Tree Fairies and Angels remains within the cottonwood tree bark for a long time. You can become part of this Universe by holding a piece of bark as you relax and concentrate. You will feel the wisdom, love, fun, and joy within.

Relics of Cottonwood Trees

How many Angels, Fairy Houses, and Wood Spirits can you find?

Printed in the United States
By Bookmasters